# The Legend of the Abominable Huckleberry

Or

"The Practically True Tale of
How the Huckleberry Railroad Got Its Name"

By Michael J. Thorp

Illustrated by Caren Huizenga

Published by
SouThorp Publishers
Flint, Michigan

Thorp, Michael J.

The Legend of the Abominable Huckleberry: (or) The Practically True Story of How the Huckleberry Railroad Got its Name / Michael J. Thorp-Flint, Michigan : SouThorp Publishers 2011. 1 Children's Book – ages 4-12

# Michael J. Thorp

*Michael J. Thorp is a storyteller and broadcaster. His first book,*
*"The Great, Great Lakes Trivia Test" was released in 2010.*
*He is the host and writer of the "Huckleberry Radio Hour,"*
*an Emmy award–winning live radio variety show produced at the*
*Genesee County Park's historic Crossroads Village, near Flint,*
*Michigan. The Abominable Huckleberry was created as*
*a character on the radio show.*

*Thorp, who earned a BA in history from the*
*University of Michigan-Flint, has been a television news anchor,*
*disc jockey and television/radio talk show host.*
*Thorp lives in Flint with his wife, Ginny.*
*They have two daughters, Libby (married to T.J.), and Ella*

# Caren Huizenga

*This is Caren Huizenga's first illustration of a book. She and au-*
*thor Michael J. Thorp met at church in Goodrich, Michigan and*
*when he decided to write a children's book he thought of her first.*
*Caren is an artist and teacher who discovered her love of art in*
*high school. She attended Central Michigan University and com-*
*pleted her BA in studio art in 1972 at Oakland University.*
*She enjoys watercolor, drawing, pottery, and mural painting.*
*Her work is in galleries and in many homes around the state.*
*Caren lives with her husband Frank in Metamora, Michigan.*

# Dedication

*For
the kid in all of us
who likes a good story,
with a little history
and
a not very scary
monster.
Perfect
for when
the day comes
that I can
read it
to my
grandchildren.*

# Crossroads Village

Crossroads Village is a real place with more than 34 historic buildings that were moved—brick, board, and stone—to the banks of Mott Lake, to recreate a Great Lakes town from the late 1800's. There is the Colwell Opera House where visitors can catch a show, like the "Huckleberry Radio Hour," it also has a 100 hundred year old Ferris wheel and a C.W. Parker Carousel.

At the Atlas Mill they grind flour for pancake mix you can buy at the general store. And, on the porch of the Attica Hotel musicians sit in a rocking chair playing old time songs. When the conductor bellows, "All Aboard", you can ride on the famous Huckleberry Railroad, with its antique wooden coaches pulled by the old 464 steam locomotive. Or, spend a lazy summer afternoon cruising Mott Lake on the "Genesee Belle" a genuine paddle wheel riverboat. But, don't forget to keep a wary eye out for, the Abominable Huckleberry. Crossroads Village & Huckleberry Railroad are a part of the Genesee County Parks based in Flint, Michigan.

# The Huckleberry Railroad

is operated by the Genesee County Parks in
Flint Michigan. It runs on, what was,
the Otter Lake Branch of the old Flint River Railroad,
established in 1857 to haul lumber, to the mills of Flint.

By 1868 the Flint River Railroad joined with the Pere
Marquette line under the leadership of Flint Lumber
Baron Henry Crapo, who was also Michigan's Governor
from 1865 till 1869. His grandson, Billy (William Crapo)
Durant lived with him in Flint and later founded
General Motors.

The Flint & Pere Marquettte Railroad got swallowed
up by the Chesapeake & Ohio, or C&O.
Later the C&O got gobbled up by the Chessie System,
which grew to become CSX.

Most think the "Huckleberry Railroad" got its name
because the train ran so slow that passengers could get
off the train, pick huckleberries along the tracks,
and jump back on with their snack.

While that is a nice story I have another, an ancient story,
a very strange story about something, purple and round,
and very big, hanging around Crossroads Village.
A story of lumbermen and store clerks, of farmers and
fishermen, who know what they saw,
but were afraid to say anything about it,

## till now...

**T**he Story
I am about to relate
is practically true,
so listen carefully
and pay heed to,...

# The Legend of the
# Abominable Huckleberry
## ☆Or
## "The Practically True Tale of
## How the Huckleberry Railroad Got Its Name"

The first to see him
was a lumberjack
they called "Crazy Bob".
He said it was
"abominable."

Crazy Bob
had been walking
along the tracks
after a long day
of lumbering.
Suddenly, at a clearing
he found himself
face to face with . . .

the **Abominable Huckleberry**,

7 purple round feet of him.

And to make it
even more terrifying the
**Abominable Huckleberry**
was smiling
and planting huckleberries.
Crazy Bob, with  a crazy
"blaahheee" sound,
turned tail, ran
and never looked back.
No one really knew
what to think about
"Crazy"  Bob's story.
But there were
huckleberries growing
along the tracks.

Others told similar stories,
but didn't tell too many, they didn't want people
to think they were crazy like "Crazy" Bob.

Years later "Weird" Ella,
a clerk at the general store,
reported seeing
something strange
while she was fishing
on a warm evening
along Mott Lake.
She said
she was stretched out
on the shore, wetting a line,
when she heard a funny noise
in the water.

There he was,
this giant purple round . . .
well it was
a huckleberry . . .
floating by.
Ella dropped her pole,
screamed "blaahheee",
and took off towards town.

When she took
a fearful look back,
he was smiling at her.

She decided not to tell anyone, they might
call her weird or something.

The whispers continued.
"Do you believe in the
**Abominable Huckleberry**"?

Some thought that those
who told the story were crazy,
others didn't know
what to think.

But everyone did know that
more huckleberries were growing
along the tracks and down by the river.

The Pere Marquette line became the Huckleberry
Railroad, when passengers got off the train to pick 'em.

Of course they were always a little on edge, they didn't want to meet up with...the **Abominable Huckleberry.**

There were more sightings;

The giant berry was
seen on the river,

deep in the woods,

and near farm fields.

Was he real?

Many
scoffed
at mention
of the
**Abominable
Huckleberry,**
but even they
were leery of heading
into the woods at night.

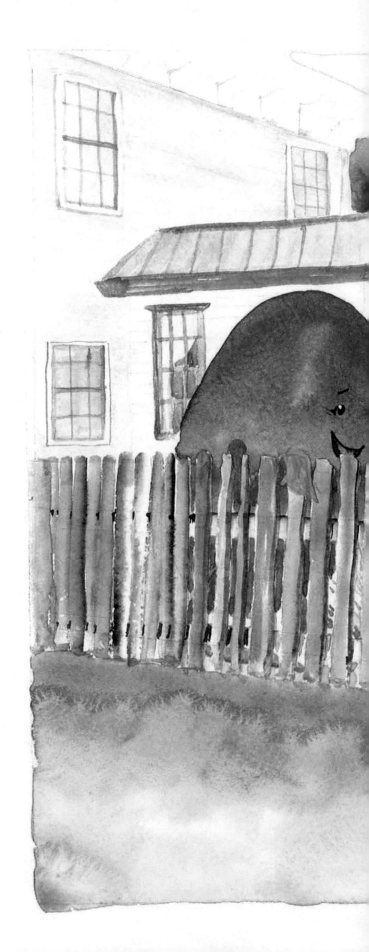

**F**inally Dave,
the Village Gossip,
was taking
a quiet walk
in downtown
Crossroads
Village...
"Drifty" Dave
he's now called.

Walking past
Dr. Barbour's office
he heard
a strange sound.
There, dancing
around the garden
spreading
huckleberry seeds,
was, a 7 foot tall
and round,
purple . . . thing.

"It's the **Abominable Huckleberry**,"
he thought as he stood there, shaking.

The
**Abominable Huckleberry**
slowly stood up turned
and looked at Drifty Dave . . .
and smiled.

He smiled?

Yes he smiled.

Drifty Dave didn't wait,
he yelled, "blaahheee"
and ran home.

But what to do? If he told anyone they would probably call him "Drifty" Dave or something!

But then he thought, maybe the
**Abominable Huckleberry**
wasn't so abominable after all.
Maybe he was just planting huckleberries.

Maybe he was why there are
so many huckleberries ...

Maybe he's why they call it the
Huckleberry Railroad . . .

So if you happen to be out
for a walk along the tracks,
or the lake, or even around
Crossroads Village
and you happen upon
a big purple thing
smiling at you,
don't yell "blaahheee" and run.

It's just the
**Abominable Huckleberry**
planting more
huckleberries.

# That's
# the true legend of the